Hunting Grounds

Krista Cagg

Dedication

This book has been a pain in the butt to get out into the world. Without certain people it would still be locked in Delay Chaos. So, without further ado, I would like to thank the following:

(In no particular order.)
My Dad and Husband
My Furry Demon Overlords
Maggie and Tray
Jen and Crystal
Kate and Benny
Chelle and everyone at Chaos
Santiago Cirilo
Midnight Syndicate
Milton, PA

If your name isn't on the list it doesn't mean I don't appreciate you. It just means my mind is busy with my make-believe people.

Love you all!

Sympathy for the Devil

"Not a bad Black Pudding, eh?"

Dr. Nathaniel B. Smythe had been lost in his thoughts until his dinner companion's question brought him back to the here and now. The scientist and philanthropist raised brows the same pitch black as his hair as he glanced at retired General Frederick F. Fremont. "Forgive me, old man. My thoughts were on the council meeting." Twenty years separated the two men, but from the day they had met seventeen years prior, the difference had never seemed to matter.

Smythe's family had a long history with the quaint, small municipality of Milltown. The only remaining member of the founding families, the Smythes had had a standing seat on the town council, status, and sway over local government for generations. It didn't hurt that they were wealthy from their investments in coal, shipping, and local industry. Nathaniel looked to be the last, however, having never married, nor sired even a bastard to inherit the family name and wealth. He was aware of the mixed feelings certain members of the town had about this. Some were eager to get the residents' attention onto a central government and council, while others felt that without the Smythe money to support it, the town would founder and die in under a decade.

Now entering his forties, Smythe was a shade over six feet tall, lithe of stature, and quiet of voice. His smooth baritone sounded out only when his perpetual mind had a solid contribution to the conversation. He was a modern man, dressed in the height of style in a tailed black evening coat with matching tapered pants. His waistcoat was double-breasted red and gold brocade, and his pressed shirt was a pristine white. The black silk cravat at his throat sported a solitary lapis lazuli cabochon, which tacked the neckwear in place. Smythe still appeared youthful with the sole exception of a streak of grey that marred the center of his goatee.

Fremont was a contrast to Smythe. The retired General was loud, boisterous and his thoughts spilled out his mouth without hesitation. Though six foot tall and broad of shoulder, the rest of the older man had the look of stout muscles gone to seed. A firm physique had softened around the edges, but had by no means diminished entirely. A lack of an active lifestyle made itself known in his jowls and cheeks. The mutton-chop whiskers and mustache hid the telltale signs for now, and his hazel eyes still held a keen spark to them. His evening wear was much along the same lines as Smythe's, but Fremont did not wear them as easily. He had a tendency to tug at his collar, hitch the legs of his pants when he sat, or rotate his shoulder. The fidgeting earned him a few looks, which he ignored with blatant disdain.

The two men were walking home from their late dinner after the monthly town council meeting, reminiscing about a time when the council wasn't as collectively thick-witted as they had been tonight. Their friendship began many years ago when

Smythe was a young man who hadn't yet inherited the family estate and businesses. He'd had wild ideas on advancing industry and radical new technology. At first, Fremont had simply been amused by Smythe's youthful ramblings. Eventually, he had recognized in the young man a kindred spirit of adventure and discovery, and he actively encouraged Smythe's ideas. Years later, after the death of Smythe's parents, they became more like associates, even meeting once or twice a week for dinner and an evening of conversation. Fremont guided the young aristocrat as needed or requested, but otherwise gave Smythe his stalwart support and companionship. These days Smythe didn't require more than Fremont's friendship. The council meeting had tarnished their standard plans for the evening. It wasn't entirely ruined, just delayed.

A small town, Milltown was founded in 1770 around a limestone mill on the Susquehanna River. The town developed around the industry as more manufactory became necessary until it spread up from the valley into the surrounding rich farmland. Most activity remained firmly in the downtown area and near the river. Churches of various denominations sprang up within blocks of each other, their spires and bell towers reaching for the sky. Original homes were upgraded with new architecture or demolished and rebuilt. Tenement apartments above businesses and offices filled and vacated with regularity as factory workers or farm hands came and went.

The citizens tried their best to create a homey, welcoming hamlet, but there always seemed to be something eerie nestled silently beneath the streets. Of course, no one spoke of it, and over time it was simply accepted as part of Milltown's "charm". Due to the ongoing silence, any speculation on the source or when it had begun was lost as years passed. Visitors that commented on it were ignored outright or politely corrected. It affected the area enough to keep out undesirables, but those newcomers that were able to live with the sensation found they made a comfortable living after being a resident three years or more. Overall, those that lived within Milltown's city limits were content, private, and pleasant if simple folk.

Fremont harrumphed in mild annoyance, his mustache bristling.

"Milltown City Council," he grumbled. "Don't know why they bother." He made a vague gesture through the air in front of him with one hand. "Useless. The lot of them. They know by now that any funds they lack in the Treasury for the proposed improvements on the gas lines will be made up by you. These…meetings…are a singular excuse for them to leave their wives for an evening of dickering that makes them sound just like the females they are trying to escape."

A quiet laugh escaped from Smythe. While he didn't share his companion's opinion of the fairer sex, he still found Fremont's description of the City Council meeting amusing. "They need something to do that would appear to be official on the surface of it or the council would be dissolved." Smythe's walking stick ticked softly against the pavement. He'd had it made to his measurements from polished ebony, and it was topped by an Egyptian scarab of carved carnelian. The carving had been a gift from Fremont, a souvenir from some expedition or another. "Then where would we be?" he quipped in dry humor.

"Drinking good bourbon at a decent

hour of night instead of after a late dinner." A grin spread across Fremont's face. The light brown mustache threaded with grey lifted up to almost above his cheekbones. His expression revealed the wrinkles at the corners of his eyes and cheeks, put there from years of exposure to all manner of climates.

This time Smythe laughed outright. His hand clapped Fremont on the back of the shoulder as they rounded the corner of Walnut Street where the steps to the front porch of his mansion were only a few feet away. "Come now. Are you suggesting that you are so aged that a mature evening with an old friend is beyond you?" He laughed again at Fremont's look of outrage.

"I will be too old for that when I am three months in my grave, you impudent boy!" As if to prove his point, Fremont stomped up the steps to Smythe's front porch. "Keep up, Smythe."

"Indeed," muttered Smythe before he followed the General with quickened strides of his long legs.

The Smythe mansion was a Richardson Romanesque Revival house. Built using local mountain stone, it was a solid block with round towers on each corner and large chimneys on either end. With two stories and an attic, it was imposing and dark. It almost seemed unwelcoming if not for the broad porch on the front of the house. It had replaced the original circular stone gazebo-like portico. The only other detail that added any sort of warmth to the structure was the Spanish red tile that comprised the roof.

Thirty minutes later, they were sitting comfortably in Smythe's private study, with a cheerful fire burning in the brick and iron fireplace. The light of the flames illuminated the intricate scrollwork around the Smythe family crest set in relief on the cast iron backing. The oak frame was carved in vertical pillars on either side, and was topped by a leaf and banner embellishment that supported the scalloped edged mantel. The maple wood frame clock that sat upon it filled the room with a gentle tick-tock. Musky smoke scented the air from the cigar Fremont enjoyed, creating a pleasant odor when combined with the subtle edge from the bourbon in the accompanying snifters.

Thick, red curtains hid the windows

of the turret in the northwest corner of the room. Smythe preferred to keep them shut day and night to maintain the privacy of his study. However, the choice did require him to make use of the gas-lit sconces on the walls regardless of the time of day. Their flames had faded the Morris and Co. marigold patterned wallpaper over time, but Smythe hadn't considered it important enough to replace the affected areas. He would simply add a painting or relic to the wall to solve the problem.

Floor to ceiling bookshelves, filled to bursting with tomes and decorations, were crafted of the same dark cherry wood as the desk that sat off to the side. A globe, an oil lamp and a book stand with Smythe's curiosity *du jour* sat on the desk top. Directly before the fireplace, he and Fremont occupied a pair of leather padded armchairs that matched the shelves and desk in masculine luxury. Round end tables of the same high polished wood sat to the right of each chair to receive the glass snifters and held marble ashtrays. Only Fremont made use of the latter.

"These meetings," groused Fremont around his cigar. The thick, blue-gray smoke obscured his face for a moment before it snaked around his head and floated up toward the ceiling. "This is what men these days have become. Meetings and pointless disagreements." Thick fingers wrapped around the cigar, which he then pointed at Smythe for emphasis. "This is what happens when there aren't any wars to fight."

Smythe set his snifter down on the table after he had taken a sip of the bourbon. His senses took idle notice of a woody aftertaste. He preferred a more sweet touch to his liquor, and made a mental note to discard this bottle. His dark green eyes glanced at Fremont as he settled into a cross-legged slouch in his chair. "Isn't your youngest son fighting the Mexicans?"

Fremont gave a derisive snort. "That isn't a real war. What kind of war could it be, shooting bandits in the desert?" He grimaced as he tapped some ashes into the ashtray. "Any fool with a gun could manage that."

Smythe's chest hitched in quiet amusement, but he did not dare voice his opinion on the matter for fear of offending his battle-worn friend. Fremont seemed content to continue anyway.

"Oh, don't mind me," he said. The base of his snifter was cupped in his rough hand, which moved in a gentle motion to swirl the liquor. "I've grown discontented in my old age."

Smythe said nothing. They had had similar conversations before. Experience told the scientist it was best to let Fremont get it out of his system instead of offering advice or sympathy. So instead, he drank the inferior bourbon while the General rambled on.

"I've fought on the field of battle, led men to victory or their deaths on honest fronts, not these ambush and raid tactics they employ now." Fremont frowned as his broad shoulders sagged. "I even retired before they forced me into it. A man knows his limits," he declared, then harrumphed. "Besides, there was more I could do with my time. Exploration was the next new thing. The discovery of lands wild and beautiful; natives with their customs gentle and terrible. New creatures to challenge a man's nerve, and I hunted them all. Bears the size of buffalo in the Yukon. The fierce and elusive tigers of India. I bagged a black maned lion in Ethiopia, and hunted with an enormous eagle on the Steppes of Mongolia." He sighed as he rested the snifter on the end table. Always an expressive man, it was easy to see that he mourned the loss of his younger days. "No longer, I'm afraid. Every land to discover has been. Every hunt done. There is nothing left for the likes of me."

Silence fell between the two for long moments. The mantel clock ticked away. The fire crackled with the occasional pop as a log split. Bourbon was drunk, and Fremont's cigar burned down to the stubborn stump of ash. Smythe could guess that Fremont was lost in his memories while his own mind turned an idea over and over, examining the facets from all sides. Any time before when he had presented suggestions or sympathy to the older man, his gestures had been rebuked, but he had never thought to propose what now came to mind. Why he considered doing so at this point in time escaped him at first, other than perhaps to help a valued friend who clearly was in need of some stimulation in his life. Though now that he thought it through, he could see a benefit for himself as well.

Smythe let out a quiet breath as he

placed the snifter down. "What if I were to tell you that there *are* still frontiers to explore, wilds to tame, and creatures to hunt?"

Fremont scowled as he scoffed. "Don't be daft, man." He punctuated his disbelief with a wry exhalation of breath. "Where? The moon? Mars?" He snickered with a shake of his head.

Smythe smiled in understanding. After all, what he was about to present was absurd in this day and age…unless you knew what he did.

"Have you ever wondered what I work on with those interns I bring in?" Smythe asked in a casual tone. Ever since achieving his majority and taking over the family estate and businesses, he had hired interns from various nearby colleges and universities. There had been many over the years, more than his businesses could account for.

"You put them to work in your business investments," answered Fremont with a roll of his hand in the air. "Those new contraptions you are so enamored with. 'Betterments for the community' I believe was the phrase."

"Yes," replied Smythe with a sly grin, "that too. But I hire more interns than the community could possibly benefit from. I have my own…experiments."

The older man grew intrigued. Smythe felt a sense of satisfaction when he saw Fremont sit up more in his chair, and look directly at him. "Experiments," the General repeated.

Smythe nodded. "I know your feelings on intellectual discoveries-…"

"They go right over my head," interrupted Fremont, but he settled when Smythe raised his hand.

"For which I shan't bore you with too many technicalities." Smythe uncrossed his legs and sat up in his chair. "What I am about to tell you must be kept in the utmost secrecy. I trust you, old friend." He didn't wait for acknowledgment from Fremont to prove that point. He didn't need the affirmation.

"Some time ago I began to experiment with alternate forms of energy in an effort to find a better, cheaper source of power." His attention went to the fire as he began his tale. "Many of my experiments failed, but that is the nature of invention. My research was my own and strange in the eyes of my contemporaries so I took on young assistants reputed for similarly odd ideas and notions. I could not manage alone. I needed fresh eyes and minds to assist and challenge me."

Smythe no longer saw Fremont. His mind played out the memories in the flames he stared at as he spoke, his voice wistful. "I had a theory about the movement of light and sound. The one always follows the other. Lightning and thunder. But what if I could somehow sync the two to happen simultaneously within the same space? Surely that would produce massive amounts of energy that could potentially be harnessed to mankind's benefit." The excitement and belief he had felt was a strong echo in his voice.

"We began our experiments using a prism and a tuning fork. It took a month to get a resonance but when we did, it pierced the eardrums of my unfortunate intern at the time. The young man will be deaf for the rest of his life." His voice was pensive and colored by lament. His mind's eyes still saw the young intern on the floor of his lab, his hands to either side of his head while blood trickled between his fingers and down his neck. He had deduced that proximity to the mechanism at the time of resonance had been the culprit, and what spared him from the same fate. Unfortunate for the intern, but advancement to Smythe and his experiment.

He frowned in renewed annoyance as he moved his hand through the air as if to wipe away that regrettable incident. "I arranged for his family to receive monthly funds for the rest of his life. They will want for nothing." Then his hand formed into a fist as it was lowered it to the arm of his chair. "But that failure taught me much. I was ready to try again, but needed a new intern as I did not wish to continue alone."

Smythe's shoulders tensed, but he wasn't aware of it. It wasn't anxiety or fear that tightened his physique, but the thrill he still felt for his discovery. "I took on a new apprentice and brought him up to date on the experiments thus far. I learned that he was a gem of an assistant when he presented me with an alternate method of achieving the resonance I desired." Fremont's groan snapped Smythe's attention to him, and the scientist smiled. He was going to go against his promise about giving details, but he could not help himself.

"We modified a Faraday disc, that marvelous piece of electromagnetic machinery," Smythe continued even in the face of Fremont's scowl of disapproval. He wanted to brag about the fabrications he had made with the machine even though he knew it would go unappreciated. "The tuning fork was attached to bracket the disc so that the sound waves would be channeled by the electromagnetism then focused on a gas pilot light. The pipe lines were run into a containment booth that we fabricated to protect us from any further violent results." Both of his hands became fists tight enough for the whites to show at his knuckles, and he delivered his broad grin to Fremont. "It worked! By God, old man it *worked*!"

Fremont's brows went up as he blinked, but he didn't look away when Smythe locked eyes with him. "It wasn't the result I wanted. The energy produced couldn't be harnessed, well not in the way I intended because I *have* contained it, but what was created was staggering." Then his expression sobered. "And frightening."

Smythe's hands relaxed, but his appearance remained haunted. "The resulting energy surge had cracked the glass of the booth wildly. The intern and I could tell something was within, so we cautiously peered inside. Chills danced over my flesh to see what we had done. Pulsing and swirling with light was a vortex of energy suspended vertically in the air, and spinning counterclockwise at a slow, steady pace. Every color of the spectrum twinkled in the bands while shadow swallowed the whole in the center of the pinwheel. It was perfectly beautiful to behold, and we stared in awe, our minds frozen on what it might be, what it meant."

Here Smythe paled noticeably, and his gaze broke from Fremont's. He was not always a proud man, but he didn't want the fear in his eyes to be seen, as he knew he couldn't contain it. The experience had scarred him just that much. He doubted that there would ever come a time when the memory didn't seem fresh enough to affect him. "Then…*it* came. The shudders of accomplishment became a cold to freeze the soul. Something…reached through from the other side. We had created a portal to… somewhere, and we had garnered attention." Smythe's hand shook as he reached for his bourbon. He felt the need of the alcohol to steady his nerves. Even now just speaking of that moment brought back the terror anew. Only after he had drunk a good portion did he continue.

"The appendage seemed boneless. It coiled on and around itself as it flailed in slow exploration of the booth. The gray-green skin shined as if slick from some terrible substance that coated its surface. Worse, taloned fingers, six in total, grasped and clawed about at the end. The click and screech whenever they encountered the walls of the booth were threatening enough to draw me and my intern from our horror."

Smythe paused to take another restorative drink, thereby draining the glass. "We panicked," he said in a stronger tone, the troubled look melting away. "I ran to the gas controls and opened the valve to its fullest while my intern tried to shut down the portal by turning off the Faraday disc. I cannot be certain which action it was that sent that horrible tentacle back, but go it did. The disc was destroyed by the flames that flooded the booth."

Fremont looked shocked and dismayed, but there was a spark of intrigue in his eyes that Smythe noted. He was relieved to see it when he glanced at the older man. It meant that the hook was set. He felt no regret.

"Am I to assume that you rebuilt the apparatus even after this alien experience?" asked Fremont.

"Of course we did," assured Smythe. He smiled in fulfillment, which earned him a hard look from his companion. He sat back in his chair again, feeling more relaxed. "We replaced the containment booth, repaired the modified Faraday disc and ran more experiments. Nothing appeared through the next portal we opened. We thought to bait something into coming by putting a cat into the booth." A smirk pulled on his lips as he huffed in quiet, sardonic amusement. "The only thing that happened was the damned feline wandered into the portal and never came back."

He refilled his snifter from a decanter on his end table. The beverage was no longer needed, just desired. "Our fear gone, we removed the booth from the equation and built a frame to contain the portal as well as dampeners so that the damaging acoustic effect would be nullified. Our trepidation may have evaporated, but our respect and good sense had not left us." He gave Fremont a wink and a clever grin then continued. "It included an iris-like mechanism that acted as a door. The portal could remain open, but nothing could come through once the iris was closed." He snorted as he lifted his glass. "Came in handy once when a voice like the Devil himself spoke to us in a language we did not recognize from the other side of the portal. We shut the iris to ensure that the owner of that tongue didn't grow too curious."

"Was it the owner of the appendage?" Fremont frowned, but Smythe could tell he was enthralled.

Smythe shook his head after he had taken a drink. "No. This was a new doorway. We found that altering the resonance by adjusting the Faraday disc's wave strength or changing out the tuning fork for a larger or smaller size produced different openings. Originally, the only way we could tell was by the rotation speed or the colors that appeared in the vortex's bands."

"Is that where your intern is now?" asked Fremont with a cheeky grin. His gave a vague wave of his hand. "Down in your lab tinkering about and shoving more alley cats into other worlds?"

Smythe's expression fell before he fingered the gray strands in the center of his goatee. They were a recent acquisition that had been remarked upon by those that knew him well enough to comment on such a personal subject. "In a manner of speaking."

Fremont lost any hint of mockery, and leaned forward in his chair. "What do you mean, Smythe? What happened?"

The scientist sighed through his nose. "He felt that after all we had done that the next logical step was to go through the portal ourselves. I argued against it. How could we be certain that the atmosphere would be habitable? The terrain solid instead of gaseous or liquid? But he took advantage of my absence one evening. I came home to find the gateway active, the iris open, and the lad nowhere to be found."

"By God!" exclaimed Fremont. He blinked for a moment then asked eagerly, "Didn't he return?"

"Oh, yes," answered Smythe with a chuckle. He shook his head, a smile pulling his lips to one side. "But not before he gave me enough of a fright to put some gray into my beard." His fingers combed through the silver streak once more. "I was about to rush into the portal when he came stumbling out. He was covered in frost, but had that look about him as if he had seen the face of God. After wrapping him in a blanket to warm him I looked him over for any damage, did a series of mental examinations but he was perfectly fine."

The General's attention was rapt. If nothing else, Smythe felt that his companion was captivated by his tale. "He lives there now, on the other side, among a race of beings that communicate solely by the mind. They research the thoughts of stars and write down their stories."

Fremont stared at Smythe, gape mouthed. "Incredible."

"Indeed," Smythe muttered. He allowed silence to fall between them again. This time the clock seemed louder, perhaps more menacing. It still chilled him at times to think of what lay dormant in his basement laboratory. More often it energized him. "I have an offer for you, old friend, if you care to hear it."

Fremont startled out of his thoughts then gave Smythe a perplexed frown. "An offer for me," he stated. His tone of voice gave weight to his incredulous viewpoint.

Smythe gave him a sober nod. "I have documented a number of dimensions. There are more than a few that would make prime hunting grounds." He arched a brow at Fremont. "For a man with the right mettle."

Another silence fell. Smythe took note of the thoughtful look that brought the older man's thick brows down. He took a drink while he let the retired explorer ruminate for a few moments, then he would continue his sales pitch. He knew he should feel some manner of guilt for luring Fremont into this, but what little remorse existed was too small to counter his desire to further the exploration of his discovery. It hadn't occurred to him before tonight that the old soldier and explorer was perfect for the next stage. Even if Smythe's cowardice made him reluctant to advance, his logical mind reasoned that it was time.

"You would be pitting your skills against creatures no man...no *human* has ever hunted before. Of course what trophies you bagged would need to be kept hidden and secret." Smythe rolled his hand in the air with a nonchalant expression on his face as if he were negotiating a more terrestrial safari.

"That wouldn't be a problem," countered Fremont. "I have a secret room behind a bookcase in my library where I keep my less than…legal acquisitions." He grinned unashamedly. "It includes a Cape Lion from Africa and a Hokkaido Wolf from Japan. Viewing is, of course, invitation only. I will show you sometime." Then he leaned forward on his chair with an intent look for the scientist. "But why?" He grumbled when Smythe arched a brow in query. "I mean, why me? You could send another intern. Hire any scrupulous explor-ah ha!" Fremont nodded as he sat back in his chair again. "I think I understand."

"You are the only one I trust, old man," Smythe confirmed with a nod of respect. "Your senses and attention to detail are keen. Reports on vegetation, inhabitants, fauna, maps of the topography whatever catches your eye would be most helpful to my research." Then a more wistful smile appeared on his face. "And you never laughed at a young man who spewed his wild notions to you when he'd had too much brandy for such a youthful tolerance. I will never forget that you always treated me as an equal, and encouraged my endeavors." He sighed after that as he rubbed his fingers against his forehead. It frustrated him to be only one person. "Also, I cannot do this alone. I must remain behind to man the controls. In case something tries to come through."

"Of course." A broad smile began to form on Fremont's face. It invigorated him, brightened his hazel eyes. Smythe was glad to see it, but he still had some caveats that he had to press upon the man.

"You would have twenty four hours," Smythe warned. "After that I dare not allow the portal to remain open to our world. For obvious reasons I would not be able to come search for you, nor send a scouting party. I cannot allow this to be discovered and fall into the wrong hands which most assuredly would happen should its existence be made known." His voice and expression grew angry, frustrated. "Some authority or another would confiscate it for so-called study, reverse engineer it then abuse it. As they do all such marvels."

"Standard exploration procedure."

Fremont dismissed the admonition with a blustering noise and a wave of his hand. "This isn't my first walk in the jungle, boy. What do you take me for?"

Smythe shook his head as he chuckled, his objection to the misuse of invention mollified. "I beg your pardon. My mistake."

"However," Fremont jabbed a thick finger in Smythe's direction. "If this goes as well as I intend I want more hunts." Then he thumbed at himself. "Just me. No others."

"Of course." Smythe smiled. Their planned endeavor excited and satisfied him. Finally, he might know what lay beyond that threshold in more detail. One day he would go himself, but not until he was certain it was safe for him to do so.

He laced his fingers together and let his palms rest on his chest as he slouched in his chair. "When would you like to begin?"

Fremont all but leaped from his chair. "Right now. Tonight." The look he gave Smythe told the scientist he should have anticipated that answer. "Let me collect some equipment from home, and we'll get underway."

Smythe was surprised for a moment

then realized he shouldn't have been. He had schemed to present the challenge to the old soldier and explorer. After years of inactivity, of course Fremont would be eager to get started. He smiled as he stood up with his hand out. "In that case I will await your return."

With a quiet slap the two shook hands.

Tally Ho

General Fremont returned within the hour having donned his well-worn safari uniform of beige light-weight cotton. The many pockets of his buttoned shirt were filled with whatever he felt was required for the expedition, while a pistol and Bowie knife were attached to the leather belt around his waist. An elephant gun was strapped over his shoulder, with additional ammunition in a bandolier across his chest. The boots he wore were of thick, stiff leather and reached his knees. No fang or claw that existed on Earth could have penetrated them easily. Obviously, he was taking no chances with the unknown.

Smythe hadn't changed his attire, only rid himself of the dinner jacket, waistcoat and cravat. The top button of his linen shirt was undone, and the sleeves rolled up. Beyond that, he remained the dapper looking aristocrat.

"Do you have all that you need?" asked Smythe as his eyes scanned over Fremont.

"As best I can tell," answered the older man with an eager spark in his eyes. "Had to guess on a few things being that this is unexplored territory, but that's the whole point, eh?"

Smythe couldn't help but smile for the enthusiasm. "Indeed." He turned to lead the way, but was stopped by Fremont's hand on his arm.

"There is a favor I need to ask of you, old chap." Smythe's brows lifted in surprise when Fremont looked him in the eyes. "I've made my wishes known to my lawyers, but in case they get squeamish I'm going to tell you. Your reputation is impeccable whereas theirs are in doubt, if only because of their choice of profession."

Smythe blinked. He knew the two of them were close friends, but he would have never guessed that he had earned Fremont's trust to this extent. "Yes, of course," he said in a hushed tone. He could do little else but agree.

Fremont gave him a curt nod. His jaw was set into a stubborn line, and he pulled his shoulders back. "Against my lawyers' advice my sons are cut out of the inheritance." He huffed in annoyance as his brows lowered over his eyes. "They're already spending plenty while I'm still alive. Neither of them will listen to a word I have to say on the matter now, but they'll damned well heed me when I'm dead!" He waved a hand through the air in a dismissive gesture. "Let the girl have it all."

Smythe's eyes widened slightly as he stared at Fremont in astonishment. His lips parted before he spoke. "The one in Danville State?" The institution was the closest and best mental asylum that followed the new Kirkbride Plan; a philosophy of "moral treatment". The treatment was more architectural in nature than actual mental therapy. The buildings and grounds were carefully designed and laid out for a more soothing atmosphere. Fremont's only daughter had been sent there years ago, but even Smythe did not know why. He thought it imprudent to ask.

Fremont's expression became guarded. "Only have the one girl."

Smythe held up a hand in a gesture of peace as he nodded. "Of course." He lowered his hand as he inclined his head toward the older man as a show of respect. "Should it be necessary I will ensure that your wishes are obeyed."

The awkward moment was brushed aside. Fremont's lips pressed together then he nodded. "Then let us begin." He clapped Smythe on the shoulder more roughly than intended.

Smythe flinched but understood. Fremont didn't speak about his daughter. To do so now and in that context couldn't have been easy for him. Smythe let the notion crystallize in his mind then let it go without further comment.

He led Fremont to the basement of his manor. Similar sublevels of other buildings were typically packed dirt floors, stone walls that wept moisture, and cubicles to store canned foods, tools, and other items not valued over much. Smythe had altered his greatly.

The stone walls were cemented over to seal out the damp and instead of one large area he had created a maze of rooms with brick walls. A turn of a knob at the bottom of the staircase brought to life the gas lights hanging from the ceiling and lining the walls in sconces, brightening the otherwise gloomy atmosphere.

There was an office immediately upon entering the basement with a library beside it. Light filtering in from the office revealed bookshelves that contained tomes that looked to be centuries old. Their spines were broken and cracked, their binding worn. What titles could be read at a quick glance made the sharp mind shiver when it realized the resources would be used in tandem. *Modern Scientific Theory, Experimental Physics, Arcane Rituals of Sumer, Goetia, Lesser Key of Solomon.* There were more, many more, but Smythe moved them along before Fremont could take note.

The pair continued on, turn after turn through the basement. Tubes and pipes lined the floor against the wall and the ceiling over their heads, all leading to a central location. They passed two small bedrooms and a bathroom then they emerged into a room that took up half of the underside of the manor. Here was Smythe's laboratory. Metal shelves took up the left portion of the room, their surfaces lined with random pieces of equipment, tubing, pipes, and tools as well as row upon row of notebooks. Interspersed among those items were jars of formaldehyde that held…things… within them. The preserved creatures were mutations of such a terrible extreme that one could not discern the animal of origin.

Smythe ignored all of it while Fremont's curiosity got the better of him. The General stopped to peer into the jars while the scientist went straight for the center of the room. Fremont followed a moment later then gaped at what he saw. "….by God."

The portal. Smythe's description hadn't done it justice. A circular dull steel frame seven feet in diameter at the aperture sat in quiet menace. The iris, currently closed, was made of the same material and spiraled like a camera shutter in the center. Tubes and wires ran along the edge of the frame to trail across the floor and to collect at a monitoring station about six feet before the portal where Smythe was busy turning knobs, throwing switches and checking gauges.

A low hum filled the room after switches were thrown in sequence. The sound was more a pressure against the skin at first, then rose in pitch into the audible range as more connections were made. Electrical snaps and pops were alarming, but Smythe didn't seem concerned by them. After a cursory glance, he paid the noises no mind.

More wires led off to the right where they connected to the modified Faraday disc. Encased in brass-framed glass, it sat on a pedestal. Smythe had kept the vertical copper disc, but had added a replaceable tuning fork above the U-shaped magnet that bracketed the disc. The whole apparatus was secured to a polished wood base, which was in turn nailed to the pedestal.

Beyond that and against the wall were more control panels with more gauges, more buttons, fuses, and switches. Gas hissed through the tubing and pipes in a gentle indication of how much of the substance was being funneled to the lab.

"No wonder you bought the gas company," grumbled Fremont as he stepped up to Smythe.

"Among other investments," was Smythe's distracted answer. He kept his eyes on the readings from the gauges, adjusting the needles with a turn of a knob here or a dial there. Finally, he threw a switch which opened the iris, and then he straightened. His eyes settled on the portal frame. Months of experimenting, fine tuning, and tests and he still felt a phenomenal pride in his creation. He always needed to take a moment before he proceeded with the operation.

Then he nodded with satisfaction before he turned to look at Fremont. "I have the resonance set for the dimension I feel is best to begin with. There is an intelligence there that would be best avoided. A plant-like entity, but they are nowhere near where the portal will open. I only know of them because of a message they sent after I had the gate open for a time. A warning, actually." He pointed to a nearby table that held an exotic looking flower growing in what seemed like a rough ceramic pot. It was protected by a glass dome. "That was sent through the portal by an unseen hand along with a book. The pages seem to be pressed hide instead of wood pulp. It contains some rather beautiful illustrations of the various flora that make up their species. They must have studied our world somehow, or their intelligence is just that vast as the notations are translated into English in the margins. They want nothing to do with mankind, so do not venture past a mountain of blue rock."

Fremont nodded. "I won't." Then he gave Smythe an eager grin. "This time."

Smythe arched a brow at his new partner in discovery. "We know next to nothing about these beings, Fremont. This isn't like the natives of New Zealand or Africa. Those could be anticipated to be human, and therefore we could have some expectations for how they think and react. But this-"

The General interrupted him with a lift of his hand. "Easy, Smythe. We can discuss it later, but discovery is what this is all about, if I understand things properly."

Smythe sighed. "You sound just like my last intern." He frowned, but he knew both men had a point. If they heeded every warning, nothing new would be created or found. "Later, then," he said as he looked back to his controls. "One step at a time."

"For now," Smythe's voice took on

a more authoritative tone as he drew down a toggle switch. A loud *clunk* came from the doorway as a gear settled hard into place then the iris retracted. "Prepare yourself."

An array of glass tubing, with jet ports at critical intervals, lined the inner edge of the frame behind the iris. Smythe turned a valve on the console and gas began filling the tube from one end. The other attached to the Faraday disc apparatus. Then he pressed a button. A clicking sound preceded the ignition of the gas. One by one, moving clockwise, the jets spouted blue pilot flames. "And then there was light," mumbled Smythe with a clever smile pulling at his lips for his blasphemy. "Now, we give it life."

Smythe moved to the right of the console and stood in front of a set of controls. He had already set the frequencies he wanted so his hand gripped the double bladed knife switch handle, paused for a moment to double check the readings then pulled it into the down position. A couple of sparks traveled down the wires from the console to the Faraday device then the disc began to spin. The arm the tuning fork was attached to shuddered as a hammer hidden within the contraption rapped against it. It set off the prongs, causing the resonance to spread along the surface of the disc.

Smythe watched it all begin to function then moved back down the console. He opened the gas valve wider, and the blue flames spewed larger from the jets. Smythe's expression grew tense, his eyes more focused, as he gave the gauges another quick glance, and then held his hand over a round button the size of his palm. His neck pulsed as he swallowed while he judged the size of the flames, nodded then pressed his hand down firmly against the button.

Another thunk echoed through the rushing and whirling cacophony of the entire machine. A channel was opened that allowed the Faraday contraption to emit the resonance-filled electromagnetic waves down the line and into the glass tubing. Smythe straightened, the thrill of expectation parting his lips as he watched the flames' brief, initial reaction to sound being introduced into the gas. They dimmed, drawn back into the tube, but it was only for the length of a heartbeat. The resonance was made to match the same speed of existence as the light of the gas flames and that was when the reaction came into being.

Fremont and Smythe both flinched when a loud, high-pitched whine filled the room. It was contained soon enough by the dampeners built into the frame of the gateway. A blinding flash of light struck them along with the sensation of being abruptly shoved in the chest. A grunt came from Fremont as he shielded his eyes, but Smythe just looked on with a broad grin on his face.

The portal had opened. Light, energy and a subtle hum slowly swirled counterclockwise. The vortex filled the frame, drawing from the gas jets to feed the effect. In the center was an opaque black eye where all of the rotating bands disappeared. Bright points of light twinkled sporadically throughout.

Fremont marveled in silence. Smythe had thought there wasn't anything left in this world that could stun his companion, but his creation had managed it. He turned a proud smile to Fremont as he murmured. "Second thoughts?"

That question pushed Fremont out of his amazement, and earned Smythe a disapproving glare. "Bite your tongue," the

General blustered. He snorted at the scientist then pulled his rifle around to double check the ammunition he had loaded into it. "Have to give a man a moment to admire his surroundings. Can't just go blundering into things. Quickest way to get dead."

"Yes, of course," Smythe agreed with an edge of humor to his voice. "At your leisure, then." He crossed his arms over his chest.

Amusement faded from him quickly, however when Fremont snapped his rifle shut then moved cautiously around the console. Smythe tracked his movement. Anticipation and anxiety fell over him. There was a small war of emotions being waged within him. The scientist said this was progress, advancement of his invention with the potential for more learning and discovery that could benefit him and, just maybe, the world. But the caring friend railed at him for sending a loyal companion into the unknown. He imagined this was how Queens Isabella and Victoria may have felt when they sent out their explorers.

"Twenty four hours, Fremont." Smythe pointed to a clock on the wall.

Fremont looked at the clock then a

pocket watch he pulled from a shirt pouch before he turned to nod to Smythe. "Twenty four hours."

The two locked eyes for a moment. Smythe realized that this could very well be the last time he saw his dear compatriot. That thought hurt, especially since he had baited Fremont into this. He would miss the old man and his vociferous ways, but he knew this would be precisely the end Fremont would want. The man had said as much on many an evening. *No soldier or adventurer wants to die languishing abed, Smythe. They want to disappear without a trace in some primeval land or by the hand of their enemy.* Those words must have echoed in Smythe's memory to have spawned this outlandish idea.

"You know my wishes," said the General, "should the worst happen."

Smythe gave him a solemn nod.

"It's all in writing." Fremont's nose wrinkled as his brows pulled down. "My boys get *nothing*."

"I understand," said Smythe.

"And our drink was the last you saw of me." Fremont pulled himself up, his shoulders squared as if the years rolled backwards on him. "I left. You went to bed."

"Of course," Smythe assured him.

Fremont pointed a finger at him with a sharp motion.

"I mean it, Smythe. I'll have no martyrdom from the likes of you. No admissions of guilt."

Smythe sighed as he pinched the bridge of his nose. No, he wasn't comfortable with the thought of a lie put towards his friend's disappearance, but it had been his own caveat of secrecy that Fremont had caught him in.

An excited grin lifted Fremont's mutton-chop whiskers as he exchanged one last look with Smythe then he turned. Gun in hand, he stepped through the portal.

Return to Camp

Smythe was startled awake by a sense of pure terror. He bolted upright in the chair near the main console where he had succumbed to the effects of boredom. The notebook he had been writing in clattered from his lap to the floor as his widened eyes locked onto the open portal. A cold sweat beaded on his forehead, his heart hammered in his chest and his lips felt parched. He couldn't immediately identify the source of his fright, but his instant assumption was the gateway. He didn't have to wait long for confirmation.

As if the hand of Lucifer gripped his heart, another, stronger wave of dread erupted from the vortex followed by a creature that made the Morningstar seem coquettish. The monstrosity that could only be described as a black demon burst into the mortal world with a screech. The sound was more akin to the protest of twisting metal than anything flesh could create. Eight feet tall, it had had to stoop to pass through the portal. The gaunt body seemed coated in shadows. Not a highlight showed on its form, and the light in the laboratory dimmed as if being absorbed by the creature. And yet there was substance to it. The cement floor cracked beneath each step proclaiming the impressive weight.

Smythe had never seen the like before. Fascination warred with frigid shock as he beheld the thing that now stood in his world. By no means a coward, he was still rooted in place unable to think rationally. Some part of his mind was aware that the monster could kill him right this moment without resistance. That knowledge told him to run, to flee as fast as he could. Hide far away from whatever devil had come through until it looked for other prey. None of it translated to his body, so he remained, gaping at the terrible alien not six feet away from him.

A head shaped like a horse's skull

pivoted on a thick neck that led to broad, but skinny shoulders. Reddish-orange points of light burned in the depths of its eye sockets, and trained on Smythe where he sat unmoving. The thing projected terror like an empathic weapon, but when it locked eyes with Smythe, vertigo joined hands with that shock. Fight or flight, neither was an option anymore, and Smythe whimpered under the effect. It lessened slightly when the beast's attention moved from Smythe to the otherworldly flower. He was stunned further when he realized that the alien seemed to recognize the blossom.

The creature's maw gaped open to reveal small, hellishly sharp teeth. What could be described as gills sported tentacles that wriggled in agitation behind its jaws. It began to lift arms that were too long. Hands that could engulf a man's head entirely ended in three long fingers and an opposable thumb, each digit possessing vicious looking talons.

The demon uttered a rattling growl that quivered the tentacles. Smythe, in his panic, thought it was about to attack or advance, but the menacing snarl cut off as the beast spun in place. It looked into the vortex then let out with the horrible screech again. A scream was pulled from Smythe as he clapped his hands to his ears, and the creature sprang into action.

The scientist expected to feel those talons sink into his flesh at any moment. That awful expectation sent his stomach spinning, threatening to empty its contents there on the laboratory floor. Smythe felt his body quake in anticipation. Never before had he been in the grip of such imminent calamity.

But worse than the expectation of his finality was the fact that it never came. He daringly opened his eyes to see that the devil was in motion, but not toward him.

It derived extraordinary strength and agility from its reversed knees on lupine-like legs that ended in oversized paws that were easily bigger than the span of both of Smythe's hands put side by side. Three toes on each paw ended in claws that the beast seemed to dig into every surface they touched. It hurdled the main control console then sank talons and claws into the wall of equipment as it gathered itself in preparation. Sounding another screech, it launched itself through the rows of shelves.

Amid the crash and clatter the demon fled the lab, disappearing down the hallway.

The overwhelming sense of fear left along with the devil. Smythe realized then that the majority of his panic had been flooded onto him by the beast. He was still on edge, however, since he flinched when Fremont came bellowing forth from the portal. He looked particularly more worn than when he went in, sporting superficial cuts and scratches with dirt and other debris that was not immediately identifiable staining his torn garments. His expression was fierce, his eyes wide and wild as he swiveled his rifle at a ready hold around the now ruined lab. "Smythe!" he shouted. "Which way did it go?!"

Smythe sprang to his feet then rushed to the damaged console. His hand slapped down on the activation button, but he needn't have bothered. The portal was already sputtering to dormancy with the equipment that operated it a victim of the escaped creature. The vortex gave one final spurt of effort and then dissolved into nothing, leaving behind an ominous silence.

Something had come through. Some*thing* was loose in their world. Smythe stared blankly at the empty gateway as panic and guilt vied for supremacy. This was all his fault! He should have shut the iris. Should have set up a knock code with Fremont to alert him when the hunt was done. Something. Now a dangerous creature with unknown abilities was loose.

"Smythe!" barked Fremont.

The shout jolted the scientist from his stupor. He looked at Fremont through the strands of his black hair that had fallen into his face. His lips moved but no sound emerged at first. He had to clear his throat a number of times before he could regain the use of his voice. "A-are you unhurt?" he asked with a tremor.

"Of course I am," declared Fremont. His eyes danced and a grin broke across his face. "You think that was something? The Punjab tigers are more daunting."

Smythe realized that his esteemed comrade was indeed having the time of his life, and he sighed as he ran a hand over his face. *What have I done?* he thought.

"But I rather think that this particular game shouldn't be allowed to roam wild through town, what?" Fremont nudged Smythe with an elbow then looked around the lab. "Bloody hell. Made a mess of things, did it?"

"Nothing that cannot be repaired," Smythe muttered, distracted. Inwardly he wasn't certain of that. He would have to do a more thorough assessment of the damage. What wasn't in question was whether he would rebuild the portal. Even now when he was fighting down hysteria there was a part of his mind that would not give up. It relegated this to the status of Set Back.

"Later, perhaps," said Fremont. "For now we need to hunt the beast down." He chuckled when Smythe gave him an incredulous look. "Yes, we. You own a gun of some sort, yes?"

"Yes, I own guns." Smythe straightened in place. He smoothed his hair back with his fingers then ran them over his shirt. They were all little gestures, mechanisms designed to gather his senses, regain his composure. They worked. His mind began to function on a logical level again instead of reacting to emotional stimulus. "I will need to change," he called over his shoulder as he made strides towards the entrance to the lab.

"Change?" Fremont's astounded

voice followed behind Smythe. "Dare I say that we haven't time to adhere to the standards of proper social attire? Not that anyone is bound to see us at this time of night," he mused. "Or so one hopes."

"I am certain that we do. I do not believe it will have gone far in such an unfamiliar environment as it has found itself in. It will be cautious." Smythe's voice gained more confidence with each step he took into the maze-like hallway. "And if I am to keep up with this hunt then I require garments better suited to the business."

"Yes, well," grumbled Fremont. "Never did hear of anyone going on a hunt in spats."

There were deep scratch marks in the floor and the bricks of the wall from the creature's flight from the lab. Smythe's eyes picked out a small, steaming pool of black liquid on the floor, and noted that the beast could be hurt. "You got a piece of it, old chum?" Smythe glanced back at Fremont as he began to unbutton his shirt.

The General gave a smug nod in reply. "It was absolutely amazing, friend! Never since my first big game hunt have I felt so...revitalized!"

"Tell me," instructed Smythe. He ducked into the small bedroom where he kept spare clothing. They were not ideal for the circumstance, but they were a sight better than dinner wear. He began to draw out individual items from a wardrobe next to the bed as Fremont told of his experience.

"Didn't have to worry about a mountain of blue rock," Fremont began. He had slung his rifle then took up a casual lean in the doorway. "Came out into a cavern of some sort. Cut stone at that, not natural, and not of any substance I recognized. Plenty of clearance over head and there was light to see by." Smythe had paused in the act of removing his shirt to look at Fremont who held up a finger. "The walls had these built in planters with vine like vegetation growing out of them. They had these beautiful red-orange blossoms whose pistils emitted a dim light the same color of the petals. It was enough to see by."

Smythe stared for only a moment before he returned to undressing. "Fascinating." He was beginning to understand his intern's desire to go through the portal and explore the worlds they had found.

"My very thought at the time," agreed Fremont with a beaming smile. "On the floor of the cavern was a stream of water that flowed toward me. Fresh water by our accounting. I tested it then began to follow the course upstream figuring to trace it to the source. Humidity built up on the walls encouraging molds and moss to grow. At certain places the water pooled, and the mosses at the edge gave off an ambient heat that wasn't entirely unpleasant. Reminded me of the hot springs of Banjar." Smythe was already half dressed in a pair of sturdy cotton work pants and had a raw cotton shirt lain out on the small bed. Fremont hurried his tale along.

"It was at one of the pools that I saw the tracks in the mud. Three toed, clawed and easily larger than my outstretched hand." Fremont held his hand out in demonstration. Smythe gave a quiet snort since those tracks now decorated his laboratory. "I pulled my weapon into my hands and continued. I tracked it upstream to an opening in the cavern where I hid behind some of that flowering ivy. There was more of it there, and I swear that it was arranged as if by the best decorator.

The entrance I lurked in had enough of the vines that it seemed a purposeful screen or curtain. With so many glowing flowers it was easy to see inside. There it was." His voice went hushed either in awe or fear. It was difficult to tell which. "Gnawing on the rotting carcass of an animal. What its meal had been in life I couldn't identify. I do not know whether that was because it too was as alien as the monster that fed upon it or it was just that deteriorated. Then I felt…fear. Like I never have before when confronted with a dangerous animal in my sights. What I looked upon was just so terrible even for a stalwart soldier like myself. I've seen visions after battles that haunt my dreams to this day, but they became childhood fears compared to this."

Smythe still felt the biting edge of trepidation from his encounter with the fiend. He couldn't imagine what it must have been like for Fremont there in the beast's natural habitat. He had to give the older man credit for his bravery. He shuddered as he pulled the shirt over his head.

"I steadied myself and sighted down the barrel at the middle of the thing's back." There was a slight tremble to Fremont's voice. "I was prepared to fire when it must have sensed my presence, for it turned. I can hardly describe it. Its *shadow* seemed as if it moved before the thing itself. I still cannot be certain that is what I saw since suddenly I was struck by a wave of nausea that rooted me to the spot. Couldn't move as the thing screamed. It was a terrible sound, like a soul being dragged to Hell. And my fear turned to bone chilling horror."

"I felt it too." Smythe had done up his pants and hooked suspenders over his shoulders. He shared a look with Fremont then sat on the bed to put on a pair of work boots. "Based on this information I believe the emotional onslaught some sort of extrasensory ability." If it was, it made this creature the perfect predator. Such an attack could incapacitate prey as well as threat. Smythe and Fremont were perfect examples of that.

Fremont coughed, which was the most anxiety Smythe had ever seen him display. "It rushed me." He shook his head. "It could have killed me easily with me unable to do more than quiver in place, but all it did was shove me out of the way." He huffed as he fingered a tear in his shirt.

"Knocked the breath out of me when I hit the wall, of course, and its claws tore up my clothing, but it also brought me back to my senses." He cleared his throat one more time then straightened, his chest puffed out and his shoulders back. "I realized it was heading toward the portal. Figured that couldn't be a welcome situation so I gave chase. I had it in my sights once. Took the shot, but it was too quick. I wanted another try, but by the time I caught up it had already gone through the portal." He shrugged a shoulder then gestured helplessly. "The rest you know."

Smythe finished tying off his boots then stood. "Yes. And now it is loose in Milltown." He started for the door, and Fremont stepped back into the hallway to give him room. "My gun is upstairs in the game room. We will retrieve it and hunt the beast together before it has a chance to prey upon the unsuspecting residents" He rounded the corner and made haste for the staircase with Fremont following a step behind.

"Bloody right we will!"

The Hunt

The demon had escaped Smythe's house through the expediency of breaking through the floor of the kitchen then bursting through an exterior wall. Water trickled from a broken pipe. Gas light fixtures hissed, but Smythe put a stop to that by shutting off the gas line to the room. Plaster painted pale lavender lay in pieces with wooden slats and broken ceramic tiles. A thick chopping block bore deep gouges from the creature's claws. A small table and chairs had been thrown to the other side of the room, and some of the legs had broken off. He and Fremont stood in the debris looking through the hole and into the night. Both had their rifles in their hands, barrels pointed downward. From their vantage point they could see that the stone wall at the far end of the garden had crumbled into the alley. Smythe sighed, but in truth he wasn't terribly upset about the damage to his house.

"Any suggestions on how to track it?" Smythe asked. Fremont was the more experienced hunter, and he had already squared off against the thing. He would bow to the older man's expertise.

"Follow the property damage, one would suppose," quipped Fremont in good humor despite the desperation of their situation. Then he pointed toward a pool of opaque, black liquid on the stairs. "And that." He stepped over the rubble, through the kitchen door then onto the small, square porch where he crouched down to touch his finger next to the puddle of blood. "There's more than my shot can account for. The creature did itself damage by not using the door." He straightened as his eyes peered out into the night. "Should make our job easier."

"Or more dangerous," added Smythe as he joined Fremont on the porch. "Injured and in a strange place amongst things it has never encountered before, it could easily lash out at everything and everyone." He glanced over his shoulder at the hole in the wall. "And it has proven that structures are no obstacle." Then he turned his attention to Fremont. "Let us hope it hasn't sought asylum in someone's house."

"Don't borrow trouble, Smythe." Fremont gave him a rough clap on the shoulder and a casual smile. "We will deal with whatever we find, what?"

Smythe grimaced at the rough strike, but hid it behind a nod. His partner didn't seem to appreciate the dire potential presented by this thing being loose in their world. Fremont's flippancy flew in the face of the consequences their lack of foresight could bring. They simply must end this quickly before they or the beast was seen. Not only could the devil wreak lethal havoc, but if they were discovered they would have to answer for their fault. It would bring attention right back to where Smythe didn't want it.

There was no use chastising Fremont, however and Smythe knew it. Better to just get on with it and swallow the offense he felt for Fremont's lackadaisical attitude. "Right." He gestured towards the garden wall with the barrel of his gun. "Lead on, then."

Fremont didn't hesitate. He took point by tromping down the stairs into the garden with Smythe following a step behind. Smythe took note that strangely, none of the plants and flowers in the pots or by the path were damaged. Some of them sported black flecks of the creature's blood, but not a leaf was missing or a stem broken. His kitchen and the garden wall gave evidence to the devil's lack of respect for building or property, but it seemed to have taken care to avoid the flora. His mind went to the description Fremont had given of the vine-like plants with their glowing flowers. Fremont had said that they were purposely planted in the walls. Smythe wondered if the beast had been responsible for that, or cultivated their growth.

They stepped through the break in the garden wall into the alley where Fremont paused. He turned this way and that before he moved off to the right, and knelt down on one knee, his rifle resting on his thigh. "Trail goes this way." He straightened then started down the alley. Smythe followed.

"Do you have any tactics in mind when we find the thing?" Smythe asked quietly. He had done some hunting in his lifetime, but that was local game: white tailed deer, black bear, and wild turkey. He doubted that the same strategies used for those animals would hold true in this instance.

Fremont didn't look at Smythe as he answered. His voice was little more than a growl in the night. "Track it fast then corner the beast. We do not have time for finesse, nor are we familiar with its natural habits to machinate a more effective technique."

Smythe was relieved to hear that despite his blasé demeanor Fremont was taking this seriously. Some of his anxiety eased to have that confirmed. "We are in need of haste, but we must be cautious to not draw attention to ourselves. Most of the town is abed, no doubt, but gun shots downtown will be heard."

Fremont snorted, and by the gaslight of a nearby garden gate Smythe could see his partner's lips press together. "Kill the thing now. Worry about a cover up later." The old hunter glanced at Smythe. "Now hush or we'll spook the game."

Smythe's brows lifted for the rebuke, but he complied. Still, his concern for secrecy nagged at him as they made their way down the alley between residences. While Fremont focused on tracking their quarry, Smythe looked at the windows of his neighbors.

Gardens and the backs of houses faced them on either side. Some had stone walls just as Smythe's had. Some were just wooden fences hastily put up for privacy instead of aesthetics. After all, who would really see it besides the help and delivery men? Not a single light was alive within any of the residences, much to Smythe's relief. It was a very real possibility they could be seen by a servant awake for the morning routine of baking bread or preparing breakfast, and have to answer awkward questions on why he and Fremont were stalking through the lanes armed with hunting rifles. He had no idea what they would say, but he was fairly certain his quick mind could invent something. It was preferable that they not find themselves in that situation, however.

Every dozen yards or so Fremont would stop, look around then continue as he spotted either another pool of the creature's blood or some other telltale sign of its passing. Fortunately, it hadn't seemed interested in entering another domicile as all of the fencing and walls were intact, and there was no sign that the demon had leaped over. He turned south at the end of the alley into another, broader alley then brought them to a stop when it opened onto the next proper street.

Smythe stepped up beside him as he looked east up the street. "Crossroad."

Fremont just grunted as his eyes narrowed. Smythe looked at him when that was the only sound that was forthcoming and saw the General glance around with subtle movements of his head and eyes. Smythe went silent and watched him work. Fremont paced this way and that then back again, lifted his chin and seemed to sniff the air. He performed every motion and gesture Smythe would have sworn was cliché to tracking except put his ear to the ground.

"That way," Fremont finally said in a flat tone. His chin jerked to indicate straight ahead of them. Across the street the alley continued.

There was a small puddle of the black ooze in the street so Smythe gave Fremont a questioning look. "How can you be sure? It could have gone east, further into town. Or west to the river."

Fremont started across the street without looking at his partner. "It kept to the narrower lanes. Stands to reason it would keep on with that given the option. Come on." He moved with determined strides. "If we lose signs of it we'll double back. Try the river. It knows water and might have fled to it as something familiar."

He kept going. Smythe had no choice but to follow, trust that his friend knew what he was doing and that the demon wouldn't escape them entirely.

Ten feet into the next alley there were no more traces of the demon's passing. Fremont stopped with a frown on his face. He looked more annoyed than worried with his shaggy brows casting his eyes into shadow, and his lips set into a thin line beneath his mustache. Smythe watched in silence as he paced in a circle, but his eyes weren't on the ground any more. They looked up and out over their heads. Smythe followed his line of sight a time or two, but saw nothing out of the ordinary. Uncertain what Fremont was looking for Smythe lowered his rifle and tucked it under his arm.

"Do not lower your weapon,"

warned Fremont without looking at Smythe.

The scientist complied. He brought his gun back to the ready, but his brows were lifted in open question.

"This is the perfect ambush location." Fremont's voice was hushed but held an edge. Only his lips moved. His teeth were clenched together. "Look, see?" He pointed with his rifle to some tall trees that hung over the alley from inside a garden. "There." The gun swiveled toward a group of garbage bins. "There."

Smythe felt the chill of fear begin to creep through his body as he looked at each location Fremont pointed out. He was certain it was his paranoia, but it felt as if those hellish glowing eyes were watching his every move. His fingers tightened around the stock of his rifle, and he swallowed against the irrational dread that tried to take hold of his mind. The silence of the dead hours of the night only added to his mounting trepidation. He expected the devil to leap at them at any moment.

Fremont turned in place to face an empty lot behind the town's post office. "And there. Come on." He rushed over at a brisk jog toward a vague form on the ground near the building.

Smythe followed with a whispered curse, stretching his long legs to keep up. Fremont reached the ambiguous lump before he did. He saw his partner's shoulders stiffen a moment before his mind pieced together what it was that lay on the ground. Smythe slowed to a walk and felt his lips part. He realized his mistake a moment later when the taste of evisceration touched the back of his throat. His hand covered his mouth as he began to cough and gag on the taste of offal, blood, and raw meat.

"Indeed," said Fremont. He was crouched down by the carcass. "Recent death is never pleasant, my friend." His gun rested on his thighs as he looked at the dead thing, the knuckles of one hand pressed next to him for balance. The head was missing entirely and what remained of its internal organs spilled onto the cooling puddle of blood around it. "Dog, looks like." He reached out to touch the remains. "Still warm. It was quick. We'd have heard it cry out, otherwise." He took his hand back then stood up. "Thing broke three of its legs, took its head and most of its insides." He turned a bland smile to Smythe. "Guess it was hungry."

Smythe choked again, and returned Fremont's look with a fierce scowl as the General chuckled, then turned to walk away from the corpse. Of course Fremont wasn't affected by the remains of the dog. He had probably seen that and worse on his hunting expeditions.

His amusement at Smythe's reaction wasn't what upset the scientist, however. Anxiety and guilt waltzed with the nausea. He feared they would not find the devil before it killed a human instead of a stray animal. Worse, some part of him feared that they would find it. The terror and vertigo that the thing had projected when it erupted into this world was reminiscent of a childhood fear of the dark. That part of a man that never quite grows up kept telling him to leave it to Fremont, go back to his lab and destroy the gateway forever if it was capable of releasing the things that went bump in the night, hid in his closet, or tried to grab at ankles from under the bed.

Smythe recognized the juvenile and unreasonable dread for what it was, and fought to push it to the back of his mind with the same strength of will he used to contain his queasiness. He would not give in to fear! Discovery and progress meant accepting the unknown, not being afraid of it. *This is only a continuation of experimentation, old boy.* He mentally chided himself. *Now pull it together and be part of the solution, not the problem.*

"Come on, Smythe!"

Fremont's command pulled Smythe out of his deliberation. He looked down the alley to see that Fremont had continued his trek south. Smythe had been too lost in his own internal debate to notice he was being left behind. With a final cough he jogged after Fremont to catch up, and pointedly did not look at the dog's remains left in the post office back lot.

The alley ended at Broad Way, the main east/west street on the north side of Milltown. It hosted one section of businesses in the downtown area. Front Street claimed the rest of the stores and offices, and paralleled the river. Broad Way was empty and dark except for the gas street lights. Those flickered in the night as if nothing were amiss, yet only broke up the dark shadows with small patches of wan yellow light. Recessed entryways to storefronts and their second floor tenements gaped in absolute blackness. Even the cast iron hitching posts along the street were ominous reminders of what they hunted. A trick of the imagination made the horse heads sprout sharp teeth in their mouths, and pin points of orange light in their eyes. It inspired apprehension in Smythe, but also revived his determination.

Large wet paw prints gave them a clearer trail to follow. Inspection of the smears revealed the black fluid that bled from the demon mixed with the more traditional color. This suggested that it carried the dog's entrails with it as it traveled through town. It was a gruesome thought, which proved to be even more ghoulish as they followed the tracks.

The traces led across Broad Way and south down a narrow side street. Just before the next cross street was a small park that boasted benches, a gazebo and a small fountain that was now flooding the grass plot around it instead of trickling as it should. The basins had been broken or knocked over. Black and red blood streaked the cement pieces.

Fremont led Smythe over to inspect

the area. His boots squelched in the mud and grass as he paced around. He grumbled in a tone too low for Smythe to understand then finally crouched down. Smythe stopped beside him, but was startled to see Fremont run two fingers through some drops of black ooze.

"What are you doing?" he hissed. "We have no way of knowing if physical contact with the creature's blood is harmful-…"

"This is fresh," Fremont said, interrupting Smythe's warning. His thumb rubbed over the ichor on his fingertips. He stood up abruptly with a scowl on his face and his eyes gleaming with excitement. His head turned this way and that as he pivoted in place. "It's still hot. We're-…"

That soul-shivering screech Smythe first heard in his lab pierced the night. Smythe and Fremont whirled to the southwest as they drew up their rifles. Perched on top of the stone wall that surrounded the Bethany United Methodist Church was the demon. It crouched like a horrific living gargoyle, glaring balefully at them. The orange lights within its eye sockets seemed brighter as it absorbed any and all light that fell upon it. Its hind claws had dug into the stone and mortar of the wall. Pieces crumbled from it every time the demon shifted its weight. The dog's viscera could be seen grasped in its large talons and held close to its body as if it protected its prize.

Fremont brought his rifle up to fire but cursed as Smythe shoved the barrel towards the sky. "No!" he insisted in a sharp but quiet voice. Smythe frowned toward the beast. "You'll hit the church."

"Who cares about the bloody church?" Fremont growled.

The demon took advantage of the moment to shriek at the two men. They cried out as a wave of dread emanated from the fiend to crash over them. Smythe would have sworn in that moment that the devil was right before them and about to sink those talons into their chests to rip out their souls. The expectation forced him back a step as his blood seemed to turn to ice. The rifle shook as his hands trembled.

Instead of what his panicked imagination foretold, the demon turned away from them. It launched itself onto the steep grey roof of the church. Slate shingles shattered from its weight or tumbled to the churchyard, knocked free of their nails. The demon then bounded to one of the medium spires on the front of the church. It grabbed the spire with its free hand and used its own momentum to swing around in a maneuver that would have put a master gymnast to shame. If not for the desperation of the situation its grace and agility might have been admirable. As it was, they lost sight of it as it dropped to the Front Street side of the building.

The night grew silent again except for the water splattering on the grass. Smythe found himself panting for breath when Fremont turned a dark look in his direction. "The church?" he asked incredulously.

Smythe took in a deep breath then let it out before he answered. "The last thing we need is an inquiry on the damage caused to the stained glass windows should you have missed the thing."

Fremont snorted with an annoyed expression. "Because the trail of black ooze and a headless dead dog aren't going to raise a few brows." His lips pressed together. "Not to mention the broken fountain, but by all means. Broken stained glass would tip the balance of bemusement into suspicion."

Smythe sighed, his patience fading. "Everything but the stained glass can be explained, and we can figure that out later." He jerked his chin southwest. "But we need to go. Now. Before it gets too far ahead of us."

Fremont grumbled, but stomped away. "Landed on Front Street. Probably heading for the river. Let's just hope it doesn't jump in or we may never find it again."

They ran across the street toward the church with Fremont leading the way. Any attempt at being inconspicuous was forgotten for having spotted the beast. Fremont and Smythe rounded the church onto Front Street where the retired General cast his eyes around for signs of the devil's passage. His main focus was across the street where the river ran quietly, its steep banks obscured by houses and offices Smythe was the one to spy the drops of blood first.

"There," he said in a brusque tone as he grabbed Fremont's arm to get his attention. He used the barrel of his rifle to point south and slightly west. "Toward the bridge."

Three blocks away stood the Milltown Bridge, spanning the eastern branch of the river. Iron lattice work crisscrossed the span in silhouette. Stone pillars secured the arches twice before the bridge connected to the island in the middle of the river. The octagon shaped glass housings of the gas lamp posts were dim, but their lights were enough to cut through the dark like beacons. Any other night, the view was peaceful, welcoming. Tonight it seemed ominous to Smythe.

With the bridge their intended destination, they jogged down the center of the cobblestone street only to come to a stunned halt a block shy. Instead of the trail continuing to the river, it turned abruptly to the west. Smythe and Fremont stood in the street facing one of the most notorious houses in town.

It was the last house on Front Street before the bridge. An empty lot separated it from the nearest house, isolating it from its neighbors. Its imposing red-sided, block-like shape was softened by the raised porch that wrapped around the north side of the house. The beige stone foundation extended above ground, and formed the wall around the porch. Stark wooden beams painted grey helped shore up the second floor with extra support from smaller beams that reached up on either side of a main pillar to form a Y-shape. The northeast corner was rounded and topped by a tower with a bell shaped roof. Next to that, protruding from the center of the roof was a grey peaked dormer. Tall, narrow windows were on either side of French doors that opened to a widow's walk. The rest of the house was plain. Even the grey shutters on the windows weren't decorative.

No one had lived in the house since it was built. The family had all died one by one, within a span of five years after construction had been completed. Nothing about their deaths had seemed out of the ordinary, just tragic. Pox. Heart failure. Consumption. And so on. There had been no relatives to claim the house, so it was acquired by the town, and put on the market. At first there had been a few interested parties, but after a single tour of the house no bids were made. After a few years even that little amount of interest ceased, and the house began to gain a reputation for being haunted. The devil's own house. Rumor had it that on the nights of the new moon, shadowy figures could be seen moving through the house. A children's dare was to ring the bell, and wait for the door to be answered. Some adventuresome youths claimed to have lasted on the porch long enough to have heard footsteps approach from inside. Even though everyone knew it was an exaggeration, their boasting lent enough credit to the ghost stories that even adults crossed the street to avoid the house even in the light of day.

The blood trail that went up the stairs to the porch was obvious, as was the broken in front door. Smythe stared at the pitch black entryway in silence for a moment then spoke without taking his eyes away from the house. "It went inside."

"That it did," answered Fremont.

"Why would it go in there?" Thus far the beast had avoided all other buildings and structures with the exception of the fountain. Based on what Fremont had described Smythe reasoned it had some affinity for water. He speculated that it perhaps hadn't meant to break the fountain. It may have just been thirsty. For the thing to decide to enter this house in particular made him wonder if there was some similar attraction within, some kindred energy that drew it. It was a ghoulish thought.

Fremont grunted in contempt. "Stands to reason. It's the devil's house."

"Nonsense," said Smythe. He turned to look at Fremont as a disapproving frown lowered his brows. Not only did Fremont just confirm Smythe's supernatural suspicions, but it suggested that Fremont himself believed in such entities. The pragmatic scientist could not adhere to the notion. "There are no such things as ghosts or goblins."

One side of Fremont's lips pulled up into a mockery of a smile. "What are we hunting then?" He grinned at Smythe then started toward the house. After a moment's hesitation Smythe followed. There was nothing to fear. They were grown men carrying powerful weapons, after all.

The foyer of the house was dark, but not enough to rob them of their vision thanks to the lights from the nearby bridge. The interior was in surprisingly good condition, however, considering that no one had lived here in decades. The hardwood floors had only a thin layer of dust on them. It was the same for the matching wainscoting that continued from the foyer into the rooms to either side. A cursory glance up the L-shaped staircase that led to the second floor confirmed the same thin layer of dirt, unmarred by the creature's tracks. The furniture that had belonged to the original owners was long since gone. Left behind were only some sheer drapes that were drawn over the windows.

The foreboding atmosphere that the house gave from without was magnified within. As quiet as the night typically was, there were always some insect sounds, or a night bird that called out. Stepping inside this house of ghastly repute silenced all of that. As well, a damp chill hung in the air. It crept along any exposed skin with spectral fingers that raised the hairs, and made one wish for the comfort of their own bed.

Fremont took a few steps further into the house then stopped. Smythe's attention trained solidly on his hunting partner. His hands held a tight grip on his rifle, and he could feel a cold sweat trickle down the back of his neck. He swallowed against a throat gone dry with apprehension. His heart pounded against his chest hard enough that he could hear the blood match the beat in his ears. Even the breath through his parted lips sounded too loud to him.

Smythe received the barest of glances from Fremont as he jerked his rifle barrel toward the central hallway then proceeded in that direction with cautious toe-heel steps. Smythe's throat clicked as he swallowed once more then followed. He wasn't quite as graceful or quiet as his partner, but he did the best he could. His feet just seemed to find that one board that creaked or his heel slid on a pool of the blood they were following, causing him to stumble. And as they crept further into the hallway the blood rushing in his ears beat louder and faster.

The ambient light from outside the house dimmed as they crept further down the hall. Smythe ceased trying to see and relied instead on his other senses. Once he switched his focus, his dread was compounded as sound, smell, and taste assaulted him. The part of his brain that was always assessing, always observing found it fascinating how details could go unnoticed until one changed their perception. It was as if the mind filtered them out until they could no longer be ignored.

Now that he was paying attention with those senses, he could *hear* from further back in the house the moist tearing of flesh, the slight guttural satisfaction from a vile throat, sharp claws rending wood as the weight on them shifted. The smell of blood and entrails permeated his nostrils and clung to the back of his tongue and throat. There was also some stale scent underneath it all, as if something had moldered in a box then was brought out after too much time contained. Smythe hadn't made the connection before, but memory of the odor when the creature burst out of the portal surfaced now. He could only assume it was the actual aroma of the demon.

When they were about half way down the hall Fremont paused just before a doorway on the right. Those terrible sounds and smells were coming from within. Fremont kept his eyes forward as he gave Smythe sharp gestures with his hand that the scientist couldn't interpret. When the General did look at him Smythe just shook his head. It earned him a bland scowl.

Fremont pointed at himself, pointed toward the door, pointed at Smythe then made walking motions with his fingers. Smythe finally understood and nodded with a helpless smile. Fremont rolled his eyes then lifted his gun into a ready position.

Smythe wasn't feeling near as cavalier about this as his partner seemed to be. The beast was cornered, but that could change in a heartbeat. It had proven itself strong enough to burst through walls. If they didn't end this quickly, the hunt could easily be renewed or lost all together. He was certain Fremont was aware of that fact, but how the retired General could seem so calm about the direness of the situation Smythe would never know.

He waited until Fremont stepped forward and put himself in the doorway. The older man swung his body and gun swiftly to face into the room then entered. As soon as Fremont was clear of the door Smythe followed, mimicking the motions to the best of his ability. Fremont had moved inside and to the right of the door to what turned out to be a parlor so Smythe went left. Then his eyes went wide.

"…oh, my god."

The dread and vertigo that the creature emitted swirled in a nauseating cyclone within the room's confines. Thus far their experience was that the sensations crashed over them in a horrifying wave. This whirlwind attack was possibly worse since it surrounded them and lingered. The thing was feeding. That seemed to make a difference in the empathic assault. Smythe felt as if the world tilted beneath him ready to drop him into a wicked abyss.

It was dark in the room, but the devil was darker still, an evil blackness that crouched in the northwest corner consuming its ghoulish prize. Small sharp teeth ripped into the entrails with a squelch, ripping chunks free of the mass. The gobbets were then ingested with sickening slurps and gulps. Pieces that didn't make it into the creature's maw fell with a soggy plop onto the floor at its feet. Smythe could see the thin but wide shoulders bunch and stretch with the action of filling its mouth or reaching for a dropped piece of offal.

Smythe's weight shifted and the board beneath his foot groaned. The monster's head snapped to the side, allowing one malevolent orange light to train on him and Fremont. The high ceiling allowed it to stand to its full height of eight feet as it whirled around to face the hunters. Its shoulders hunched as it took in a deep breath then let out a blast of that nerve shredding screech. The arsenal of terror it used was unloaded fully upon the two men just as its legs bunched. Half a moment later it launched itself at them, overlarge hands splayed open on outstretched arms so that its talons would catch and rend first before it would sink those vicious little teeth into them.

Two rifles barked out almost at the same time. Smythe felt his back hit the wall behind him just before the demon landed with a heavy thud between him and Fremont, its horse skull shaped head in the doorway. As he panted for breath, his eyes wide, he saw the blackness release like vapor from around the creature. It drifted up into the air. Smythe could swear that there was sentience in it, glaring at him, hating him with every ounce of its being. The malice emanating from that dire cloud was absolute. Then, just when Smythe thought his blood might freeze in his veins, it evaporated with an audible sigh.

He closed his eyes as he tilted his head back against the wall to catch his breath. It felt as if his heart were going to burst inside his heaving chest. The image of the creature leaping for him was burned into his mind's eyes. It took a mantra from his childhood to push it to the back of his brain. *It is just my imagination. It is just my imagination.* He had just begun to manage some semblance of calm when Fremont's voice shattered the silence.

"Well done, man!" Fremont was blatantly pleased.

"For the love of god, Fremont," Smythe breathed as he bent over, his heart back to a rapid pace after that. "Shut up." He sucked in air a number of times as Fremont laughed at him. He was beyond caring about his dignity now.

"When you're done reclaiming your manhood have a look at this." The General sounded unrepentant, but inquisitive.

Curiosity pried Smythe's eyes open and straightened him from his crouch. Fremont knelt down next to the body of their prey. The sight of it formed a thoughtful frown on Smythe's face, and he pushed away from the wall to join Fremont.

It truly was worth a look. The shadows that had pulled free upon its death had been a shell of some sort. What was left behind was a pale grey corpse much thinner than it had been when alive. It seemed to be nothing but skin pulled tight over sinew and bone. "There is no muscular structure to speak of," said Smythe with wonder in his voice. A glance at the head added to his amazement. "Nor eyes, apparently." He squatted down. "Look," he said as he nudged the cheekbone with his rifle barrel. "Empty and the sockets look burned." Indeed, there was a charred quality to the skin around the eye sockets. "I wonder what an autopsy wou-…"

"Bugger that, Smythe," Fremont interrupted in a sharp tone. "This is *my* trophy. You want to be present for the taxidermy you're welcome, but no tinkering around with the carcass."

Smythe looked at Fremont petulantly for a moment then nodded with a tired smile. "Of course, my friend." He would take Fremont up on the offer to attend the stuffing and mounting of the beast, however. "We should move it now, though. The sun will be up soon."

"Right," Fremont agreed. He stood up to sling the rifle behind his back then nudged the beast with a boot. The body moved more easily than expected. "Huh. It's lighter."

Smythe shouldered his rifle then gave the remains a shove. It rolled onto its back without much effort. Two large holes graced the thing's chest, one where a heart could be assumed to be, the other a foot to the right of that. They were just holes, however. No black fluid oozed from the wounds. "No blood either." He looked up at Fremont. "Those shadows…they must have contained every bit of life it had." His attention went back to the now entirely innocuous being. "Fascinating."

"Fall in love with it later," quipped Fremont as he moved to the head of the beast. "Grab its legs." He positioned himself to lift the torso with his hands under its shoulders. Smythe complied then together their hoisted the remains from off the floor.

"We should leave through the back," suggested Smythe. With the creature's legs under his arms, he found the position a bit obscene. The thought showed in the thin line of disapproval on his lips. "Follow the river back to your home. Less chance of us being seen by early rising servants that way.”

"Suits me." Fremont didn't seem to be enjoying his end any better. The large head ended up rested against his chest and the side of his face as his arms hooked under the creature's shoulders. "Got a door to the basement behind the house. We can take it straight down." At Smythe's querulous look, he grinned. "I do my own taxidermy. You aren't the only one in town with a lab in their basement, son." He grunted as he adjusted his grip on the corpse. "Honestly. The one we have in town is a thief. One hundred dollars for a leopard? Robbery, I tell you. The cur began to raise his prices the more safaris I went on, too. Steady now." Fremont began to walk backwards to allow Smythe the easier path.

There were a few graceless moments before they were able to coordinate their movements. Smythe had to release his hold to open the back door. Fremont then pulled the body down the stairs where he waited for Smythe. The empty house didn't boast a garden or wall on the river side, which made beginning their trek convenient. Smythe regained the legs of the creature then they descended into the brush of the river bank. They reasoned that if they kept close to the river it was less likely that anyone would see them what with the bank so steep. The trees would help obscure the view as well.

There were mumbled curses from both men along the way. Their clothing and rifles seemed to catch on every branch or bramble. One or another of the beast's arms would fall from its chest to drag the ground before Fremont would be able to achieve solid footing and replace the appendage across the torso. They hadn't considered the mud and rocks that made up the edge of the river bank either. If not for their boots they both would be nursing twisted ankles for the next few days.

The sky was beginning to lighten in the east when they reached Fremont's house. The musty smell hadn't dissipated with the beast's death, and it permeated everything. Smythe planned on burning his clothing after this. Between manhandling the corpse and the hunt, he was desperate for a bath, but he was also exhausted. He wasn't certain what he wanted more, to be clean or to sleep for twelve hours straight. A grunt escaped him as they crested the top of the river bank

into Fremont's garden. "None too soon."
He frowned as his black hair threatened his
eyes.

"No one said hunting was a casual
sport." Fremont looked sweaty, but still full
of vigor. Smythe momentarily felt a bit of
hate for his friend.

"Yes, well I think I will swear
off Black Pudding after this, my friend."
Smythe was almost of the opinion to avoid
meat all together now.

Fremont's garden did have walls,
but not on the side facing the river. Smythe
had asked him about that once. Fremont's
answer had been that there had once been
a wall, but he had it knocked down so he
could see and access the river. He liked to
sit on the bank some soft evenings to watch
the fireflies dance above the flowing waters.
He also enjoyed fishing. There were rumors
about great aquatic beasts that swam in the
depths of the river. They could grow to over
seven feet long, and sported long, sharp
fangs. Fremont was determined to catch one.

A brick path led straight through
the garden with herb boxes lining one side.
The other was bordered by colorful flowers:
Foxglove, Day Lilies, Bleeding Hearts and

Marigolds. In the center of the garden was a fountain crowned with a carved marble statue replica of the Birth of Venus. Stone benches rested at the compass points near the fountain and the path encircled it.

Fremont led them to the side of his house near a work shed. It was the older man's turn to set the carcass down as he needed to unlock the shutter doors that opened to the basement of his home. The jangle of his keys seemed louder to Smythe. He flinched before looking about them then recalled that Fremont's cook didn't live on the premises, and wouldn't arrive until at least an hour after sunrise. The retired General enjoyed a later morning than others.

The doors were propped open within a few minutes then Fremont hefted the lifeless form back into his arms. He guided them down the stairs where they had to stop again for him to turn on the gas lamps. In the center of the room was a large metal table that rose to a height of four feet. Fremont led Smythe to it, and together they levered the devil onto it.

Smythe let out a breath as he fingered his hair out of his face. He was only partially successful since a lock of it fell back onto his forehead, but at least it was better than it had been. All though he was tired, his curious mind still took in the details of Fremont's taxidermy lab. The table they had placed the beast on sank in the middle and had a drain that emptied into a sewer grate in the floor beneath it. Another smaller table on wheels sat at the head of the examination table. Various sharp implements were displayed in some order that Smythe didn't recognize. Some of the knives were large enough to butcher meat from the bone. A wooden work table was against the wall. Some small bundles of cotton and clumps of straw littered the table's surface. Above it were rustic wooden shelves that contained boxes, rolled cotton, and jars of chemicals both powder and liquid. Chemistry was not Smythe's area of expertise, and since Fremont apparently didn't believe in labeling the jars their contents were not immediately recognizable.

Smythe let out with a loud breath as he smoothed his hair back with his fingers. "Have you given any thought to what we might tell the authorities?" His head already hurt at the thought of explaining the evidence left throughout the downtown area.

"They will no doubt seek one or the other of us out."

Fremont nodded. "Bear," he said succinctly.

"Come again?" asked Smythe incredulously. His mind went to the size of the tracks, the black blood mingled with the dog's.

"Why not?" Fremont gave a blithe shrug. "We say we spotted it on our way home from the meeting. We retrieved our guns and hunted it ourselves. These ninnies will believe anything you tell them and I am the authority on game. The color of the blood could be blamed on disease."

"And the strangeness of the tracks?" Smythe crossed his arms. "It had three toes, man."

"Mutation isn't unheard of." Obviously, Fremont had been giving this some thought. "Consider those creatures in the little jars in your laboratory."

A tired chuckle tumbled out of Smythe as he held up a hand. "I will follow your lead, my friend." He looked at the creature on the examination table. "I think I'd have rather faced a mutated bear."

"Going to have a hell of a time

building a frame for this thing," grumbled Fremont. "Think I'll need stronger wire maybe. Lots of it."

"A puzzle for another day, my friend." Smythe turned a weary smile to Fremont. "For now I think I shall take to my bed and dream of a place without shadows and disemboweled dogs."

Fremont chuckled again then came around the table to Smythe, his hand held out. "Get your rest. You'll need it to repair that machine of yours." He grinned when Smythe blinked at him in confusion even while shaking his hand. "This was a good hunt," he continued by way of explanation. "Have to go again once I get this beast stuffed, mounted and on display in my secure collection."

Smythe's brows came down. His fingers combed through his goatee after he released Fremont's hand. "I thought perhaps you might not wish to after this." Not repairing the portal had only been a fleeting through in his mind. There was too much to learn, too much to explore to allow the gate to remain destroyed. Smythe had simply assumed that Fremont may have been satisfied with this single botched hunt.

"Nonsense!" explained the older man. "This was stimulating! It put life back into these old bones. Want to see what else there is."

Smythe's answering smile was faded at the edges. "Yes, of course." He put a companionable hand on Fremont's shoulder. "I will endeavor to put it right as soon as possible."

"Excellent, my friend." Fremont beamed a smile back at Smythe that made the scientist even more tired for seeing it, then began leading him toward the shutter door entrance they came in. "I will send a message when I am ready to begin the taxidermy. Probably tomorrow evening. Late. After the servants leave."

Epilogue

Fremont saw Smythe out of the basement with a few more exchanged pleasantries that Smythe wouldn't remember. It was only a short block and a half to his mansion from Fremont's home, but his mind turned the night's events over and over during his walk. He concluded that Fremont was an invaluable asset to his research. Yes, there had been mistakes this time that could have ended with far more tragedy than one dead dog and a broken fountain. Next time he would close the iris after Fremont entered the portal. They would arrange a coded knock to alert Smythe that the hunt had reached a successful conclusion. The fact remained that advances had been made, and Smythe now knew more about that dimension than he could have hoped for in sending his old friend.

One, the creature had a rudimentary intelligence. It preferred to flee rather than attack until it had been cornered. This suggested that it wasn't merely the destructive and terrifying beast that its appearance implied. It valued life over killing. Instead of attacking them at the park, it had warned him and Fremont before it fled again.

Two, now that he wasn't faced with it, Smythe admired the abilities that the fiend had displayed. The empathic assault was enough to petrify a man in place. With the vertigo and nausea added to it, the monster was assured a prey that was not going to flee, nor would a predator give chase easily.

Three, the shadows that had encompassed the creature while it was alive was an intriguing mystery. Smythe wanted to know more. The dark vapor had seemed to recognize him before it dissipated. He would swear to it.

On top of all of that, the only actual violence it offered was to the dog, and that had been for a meal. Smythe recalled how he

had taken notice that not a single plant had
been disturbed or damaged by the thing. It
made sense when coupled with what Smythe
knew of the sentient plant beings of that
world, and what Fremont had described with
the flowering ivy in manufactured planters
on the wall of the cavern. Perhaps this
demon was affiliated with those floral minds.
Fremont *must* return to that world one day!

As lost in his ruminations as he
was and affected by his fatigue, Smythe
neglected to notice a scrawny and
bedraggled crow perched on the roof of his
porch. It tilted its head with an awkward,
creaking movement as it watched the
scientist with eyes that glowed red. Smythe
ascended the stairs then opened the front
door. The crow clacked its beak together
once before it took wing from the porch
roof. A dour woman in black stepped out
from behind a walnut tree that graced
the front yard of the house across from
Smythe's. The crow flew unerringly to her
where it took up roost on her shoulder as she
began to walk with determined strides across
the street.

Fingers so slender as to be skeletal
bunched into the long skirt of her demure

dress to hoist it as she marched up Smythe's porch stairs. The same hand then lifted to rap against the door frame. She could see him through the beveled glass with its decorative etched scrollwork. He had just begun to climb the stairs to his second floor. She knocked again more insistently and was satisfied to see him hesitate. As he returned to answer the door she folded her hands together at her waist. The crow began to preen strands of her dark hair from the tight bun in which it was wrapped. This close she could hear the gears and cogs turn and click within the feathered body.

Smythe frowned as he looked through the window. He opened the door with that guarded confusion so recognizable on his face. "Jane?"

She thought he looked horrible, hair in disarray, dark circles under his red-rimmed eyes, and he smelled atrocious. Jane's nose wrinkled as she looked up at the man she had so wanted to marry all those years ago. "Nathaniel." She lifted her chin. "I know what you did last night."

About the Author

Krista has come full circle in her life. Born and raised in a small town in Pennsylvania, she moved to Savannah, GA after she graduated from art school in New Jersey. From there she moved to Olympia, WA…then back to Savannah, and ultimately back to Pennsylvania. She lives near her father with her husband and four furry demons (cats). For fun, she cultivates her squirrel army in the backyard.

As an active pagan for many decades, Krista has come to understand that there is more to our natural world than meets the common senses. She lived with ghosts inSavannah. Seen things in the thick forests of the Pacific Northwest. Investigated hauntings in Pennsylvania. There may never be a time when Krista doesn't look for the undiscovered.